More Praise for Show Her a Flower, a Bird, a Shadow

With precise beauty and unsparing wisdom, Peg Alford Pursell shows us "Anything can happen: anytime." The dead resurrect in fragments of memory, kindness is necessary courage, lives dissolve, reshape, renew, and another's hand will imprint on us its lesson in brokenness or its blessing of love as we fly into and out of the cages of our temporal selves. *Show Her a Flower, a Bird, a Shadow* is a small but fiercely sacred book, immense in its gifts.

—Melissa Pritchard, author of *A Solemn Pleasure* and *Palmerino*

I've always firmly believed that the amount of words a story contains has zero to do with how much weight the story carries. Peg Alford Pursell's new book, *Show Her a Flower, a Bird, a Shadow*, proves this once again, and proves it in spades. Read "Circle" or "A Lot to Learn" or "The Girl in the Picture" or "My Descent"—and many more—and you'll see what I mean. These stories are like gut checks to the soul.

—Peter Orner, author of *Love and Shame and Love*
and *Last Car Over the Sagamore Bridge*

"Peg Alford Pursell writes beautifully and evocatively about both the world around us and the one within. Her prose is spare, her observations keen, her heart fully on display. *Show Her a Flower, a Bird, a Shadow* is striking debut from a great new writer."

—Tom Barbash, author of *Stay Up With Me*

Reading this book is like walking through a snowfall of petals—and thorns. There is a light airy feeling to Peg Alford Pursell's delicately worded fragments that is seductive, at first, until you realize that each swirl contains small stabs of loss and pain and violence. A really beautiful, unique collection.

—Molly Giles, author of *In All the Wrong Places* and *Iron Shoes*

March 27, 2017

Marisa,
    So looking forward to our
conversation about these
pages, and so appreciate
your interest.

Show Her a Flower,
a Bird, a Shadow

Yours,

Peg

Peg Alford Pursell

Copyright © 2017 Peg Alford Pursell

Copyright © 2017 Cover Art "White Dove and Roses" by David Kroll

ELJ Editions, Ltd. ~ New York

ELJ Editions

Library of Congress Control Number: 2017932584

ISBN 13: 978-1-942004-28-8

for Cass
for my family

CONTENTS

Something freshly birdish
starts rustling in the reeds.
I sincerely want them
to hear it.

"Parting with a View," Wislawa Szymborska

Day of the Dead

When I was a child, Day of the Dead meant sugar skulls, staying up past midnight, marigolds, burning copal, blazing votives. I didn't recognize any of the faces in the photographs on the altar. Now I have my own dead—and no sweet bread, hot wax, or tequila to lure them, no fancy *papel picado*.

The dead come anyway, in fragments, perforated memories. My grandmother wearing a man's fedora, a secret greeting card folded into her dress pocket. My grandfather, who burned *basura* in his basement fireplace sending obscene odors throughout the neighborhood, whose last act was to eat a bowl of strawberry ice cream in the middle of the night. The crush I smoked pot with behind the brick chimney in the attic of his parents' home, wrapped up with me in his sleeping bag. He confessed he had no plan for after graduation, and he laughed, and he never needed the plan. The stillborn girl, who looked like a baby bird with bulging eyes, curled in a nest under the acacia. The man I'd once thought was the one, who wasn't, and whom I couldn't live with once I understood that, who on a tear of amphetamines put a gun to his head.

The dead. I want a belly of bravery. I want to know the kindness sent out of the cage of the heart. An eye that never becomes insensate to the invisible spectrum, an ear that never dulls to the song of the pulse. The night grows long until it's short, and the sweetened tongue kisses the breath, and the breath is the breath is the breath.

Dislocation

The girl arrived in a wooden crate, fighting the space for air with moths. Her belly swollen, yet empty. Tiny mouth askew, not the same as mine. I once loved the smell of sawdust. He takes her down the hall. His wedding ring glimmers. They retreat to the spare room with shelves of unlabeled green bottles, the high window of colored glass glinting like blood. I go outside to study. Broken pieces of language from the guidebook. Sit on the curb in the baking light. At my side the pocketbook he got me at the farmers' market, a diamond pattern etched into the strap. I try to feel only my concentration, desire for success. In spite of the heat, my mind frozen. The bird's white wings blur in the sun.

I Don't Want to Talk about Valentine's Day.

I don't want to talk about Valentines. Stand there by the dark window and look at me, your eyes clear as water, clear as that stream down behind the house, into where, when you last said you wanted me, you coaxed me, a downy green day, fog in the fen, vapor rising from the stones along the creek bed. Imagine the smooth cool of those stones on your back. They were under mine. Through the oaks a few straggly rays of light broke. I'm going to pour out this pitcher of water that's been moldering in the refrigerator since spring before last.

I don't want to talk. I want to run my fingers up the ridges of your spine, that trail stretching the skin that seems to say we are perhaps equal in the way that we are made of the same materials. I want you to feel my fingers, to deny fears that may form as my fingers pause at each vertebra. I want you to think of crayfish stuck in the eddying of the stream, caught, caught again, again, waiting for a change in the water.

I don't want to. What? Remember your laughter like the sound of the creek, the trees, the stones.

I don't want.

I don't.

The Map She Is Trying to Follow

She's been making some difficult paintings using yellow the shade of an aged claret. A granted favor, these interludes of solitude, the brush in the hand with its compass, this color like a chalice of bees. Her life after childhood stands as in a closet or under the bed, unknown revelation, ambition. Someday she will look deeply enough to recognize herself in the clouded mirror of shame. The map she is trying to follow is the back of her hand. There is an arrogance in assuming that you belong where you choose to stand. The artist and the world must strike some compromise. Perhaps she is a window, the open glass of every looking eye. Or perhaps the dreams of those who sleep on top of her like the pale fish of ancient rivers. Perhaps the light of the rounded air that shines on the missing in the meadows of yellow silence. Sometimes the sun seems a perpetual noise.

At the Flower

An answer eliminates all possibilities but one. Just as in marriage. He didn't believe in stopping, resting, or pausing. Drive was everything. Look at the fat bumblebee busy on the flower stalk: the creature anything but in repose, gathering nectar for all it's worth before moving on to the next. That was how to be in the world. He hadn't made himself up. He was the animal of some other's making. His was simply to follow his nature.

Petal, Feather, Particle

Show her a flower, a bird, a shadow, and she will show you what is simultaneously forming and falling apart. What is both witness and sign along the way on this rough earth, a shell already cracked. She'd thought she could raise a child with only minimal intercession but now, as she was being driven to the hotel, found herself looking up at the ceiling of the car, mumbling a quiet prayer. Her daughter was like her: too quick to do everything.

The girl's father had been someone she once knew, or thought she had, a man who laid her in repose on the bed and gave her waist a tender squeeze before arranging her hands on top of her, placing the right over the left, palm over knuckles. He studied her in that corpse-like pose, letting his glass with the float of lime warm in his hand, before his mouth captured hers.

She'd come in from that life long ago, to cover child rearing herself. To say that she had managed well would be to deny the truth of the flower, the bird, the shadow.

She would try to give her daughter a talk, though surely the young woman too understood there is nothing available to speech, the wild and strange language that could reveal the organizing principle that pulls the body toward its center. This trivial fact of human nature. Composition and decomposition of every petal, feather, and light particle.

But it was only kindness, necessary kindness, that she try. And so they were scheduled to meet in the hotel by the harbor, a place where she thought the sea would soothe her, where she would set out to speak in the way gondoliers push their boats away from the Venetian docks.

A girl in trouble: the expression implied that the girl was in danger, contained her own peril. She would make clear to her daughter that this wasn't so. Now she wouldn't likely become a famous dancer in Russia, she would say to her girl, and they would share a small smile at the idea that her daughter might have ever entertained such an aspiration.

What her daughter had ever wanted she truly didn't know, and that knowledge was contained within her, a small sunken place, heavy and aching.

It was not too late to learn, she reassured herself, but was this simply another beautiful idea she was still trying to believe? And if so, where was the love in that?

The car pulled up in front of the hotel with its grand façade. She wanted to cry out, fly toward the glittering ocean, a rose gripped in her hands, petals littering her shadow as it disintegrated over the deep waters.

Girl on a Hobby Horse

When my romantic relationship of fourteen years broke, I learned many new unnecessary things. The way dust accumulated in a pattern on the floor of the empty closet. The variations of silence, how stirring the long-handled spoon in the soup pot echoed in the kitchen. The scent of the shower water bereft of the man's soap.

Though a psychologically literate person, I didn't know what my actual feelings were. Yet I wanted to hold onto something from those burned-out flames of desire.

In an illusion of coincidence, my grown daughter returned to stay with me while her apartment building was being renovated.

Always things coming together and falling apart, she said.

Her head shaved, she dressed in saffron and crimson robes like a monk and her skin emitted a glow. She wore a look of bewilderment that didn't express her personality. I remembered her as a girl riding her stick horse through the hilly yard, galloping on her own two feet, her flame of hair in a tail behind her.

Only dogs and babies love unconditionally, she'd once said.

She moved into my sewing room and created a pallet of thin blankets, where she slept, upon the hard floor. The days passed; her round cheeks thinned and grew pale. She carried bruised bags under her eyes, dark eyes that burned in her face.

We had in common a strong meditation practice, mine perhaps

stronger only by a longer history, and we experienced the same vanishing of time as we sat. But lately I had begun to doubt the veracity of the practice. I no longer experienced a sense of oneness with the universe.

One morning I came across her outside sitting in lotus, the white arches of her feet gleaming in the dawn, her long eyelashes resting on her cheeks like flickering shadows.

All day she would sit in the garden.

I was filled with desire for such certainty as she.

I would not meditate, I decided, and each hour my refusal strengthened.

Late afternoon I tried to nap. When I closed my eyes I discovered I could barely remember what my ex looked like. Behind my closed eyelids, objects appeared as streams of particles disintegrating. Everything decomposing.

I rose shakily, a sudden need to make sure of my daughter.

At my approach she sat blinking mildly at the streaked purple clouds, the rose bushes flaming in the setting sun, the evening sky shutting down around her.

She spoke to say she loved me, a deep crack in her voice.

I saw the truth of her loneliness, of her striving to banish desire. We were the same and different, fearing what drove our animal selves, and we neither loved unconditionally nor maybe even knew how to live as loving beings.

I placed my hand on hers, her tender parched flesh stretched over bones. She made a sound between a sigh and a repressed sob. I wished it would rain, to quench something.

She Wanted

to be the girl who came into the restaurant where her family waited to celebrate her and when she entered they each would say *congratulations*.

And many would mean it.

At least one.

Three Notes to Dear Miss _____

One.

Dear Miss _____,

You were the subject of discussions in our household. You of the inky black hair (dyed) that curled under in a uniform roll, the dark-framed glasses that made you look grimmer and more removed than surely you were. You weren't the hardest—by which I mean the most unpleasant and unforgiving—of teachers. You seemed to possess some softness, or at least a willingness to bend a little. Warmth? No. You'd also been my mother's teacher, and because of that my parents were convinced you didn't care for me. The implication: my mother wasn't likeable. I was supposed to take that as fact, unquestioningly, and I did.

I carried with me the knowledge that I was an inferior student, of an inferior people. It didn't matter that I was smart, my grades high. My inferiority was as much a part of me as were my two feet that carried me up the snowy sidewalks to the schoolyard where I stood waiting for the bell to ring, my breath freezing in tiny clouds.

As much a part of me as my hands, meant for keeping to myself, folded on my desktop when not gripping the yellow pencil correctly to form words I copied from the board onto my tablet. My back-end seated properly in my chair to serve as the foundation for good strong posture, eyes directed straight ahead.

At home I received other lessons.

You would not want to know.

But you did know, didn't you? You knew without knowing the details. The head drooped over the book, the way a kid can't look you in the eyes.

The tiny, jagged white scars that marked her forearms.

You knew my inferior mother (and her mother before her).

Sincerely,

A former student

Two.

Dear Miss _____,

This is the good incident I remember about second grade though it is more about Dad than about you. You were only the catalyst. The episode took place the first day back after Christmas vacation. (It was okay then to use the term "Christmas vacation.")

Just before the bell rang to go home, you distributed little white envelopes onto the students' desktops, thank you cards for the gifts you'd received from us.

Before the holiday, we students had stacked our offerings under the classroom tree that we'd decorated with colored paper chains and lacy white snowflakes, ornaments we'd folded and cut and pasted for weeks. What a heap of sparkly gifts for you! Which you did not open. Some children were disappointed. Ronnie O. slapped his desktop and then put his head down when you spoke to him sharply. But you were adamant and did not unwrap a single present.

Who knows what my gift was? Something my mother had selected from the five-and-dime, inexpensive but costing more than she cared to spend. Teachers' presents were an obligation, however, and important for what they said about the giver—that was her position. Purchasing them was as much an anxiety for her as a duty. My only involvement was to deliver the wrapped present to the class-room.

I tucked the thank you card into the pocket of my bookbag to carry home, and that evening at the dinner table passed it proudly to my father. What a beauty it was: thick white paper embossed with silver lettering in fancy cursive, the way I longed to write. I wanted to thank you for your card.

"Wouldn't it be funny if you did," my father said, "and then she gave you another thank-you for your thank-you? And then you thanked her again, and she thanked you again!" His face wore a bright expression.

"No!" The word burst from my mother. She was very clear a-bout what a breach of etiquette that would be. I was *not* to thank you for your thank-you card.

Dad's smile faded and he said, "Your mother's right."

And that was new, and strange.

In the window the sky had darkened to twilight, a frosty shade of blue-gray I liked, and snow had begun to fall again. In the distance a few lights glowed yellow in faraway houses, the homes of classmates.

In the silence, forks scraped on the plates.

Then Mother began talking, her voice high and edgy. She chattered and laughed. I understood then that Dad's easy agreement had surprised her, too.

Soon Dad pressed his paper napkin to his mouth and pushed his chair away from the table. He handed the thank you note to me as he left the room. He winked at me.

Sincerely,

A former student

Three.

Dear Miss _____,

This is the bad incident of second grade. You went out into the hallway to talk to Miss Meyer. The two of you often met in the corridor outside your classrooms and spoke in quiet voices about what we, the class, could never hear, though we strained our ears to do so. That day, as usual, before you left the room you tasked us with completing a worksheet—probably adding or subtracting numbers—in pungent purple ink that still may have been damp, as occasionally the mimeographed papers were. Sometimes we smart students would finish our worksheets before you reappeared in the classroom. Like that day.

You were furious when you stepped back into the room and saw Mark Ivers trying to remove a thumbtack from the sole of my shoe, my leg stretched across the aisle to him, my foot in his hand.

"Put your leg down, young lady." In a few quick strides you stood between us.

Shame flooded me instantaneously—for what I didn't know.

A perverse idea in your imagination, I later decided, the memory returning to me time and again. I tried to make that idea all about you, not about me, not about how it seemed to indicate a kind of idea you had of me. Me in a yellow cotton dress, white knee socks, black and white saddle shoes, the scuffed toe of my shoe in Mark Ivers' hand. *Young lady.*

And you, Miss _____. Your voice, your voice, your voice.

Sincerely,

A former student

Circle

The day after her eighth birthday, her father said he was going to break her. Can you give him any more sympathy if you understand that's how it was in those times, that, before him, his own father had seen it as his duty to break his child? Humans were simply another species of animal, and in order to make it in this world, you had to be able to shoulder a yoke.

For a time, every day after supper he beat her with his belt. He was going to straighten her up, he said. She was evidently crooked. She was something that caused a father a lot of grief, the kind of father who was just trying to make it in this world, the kind of father who'd been half-broken himself. *You think you will not cry?* when he was beating her, he said.

To appease him, to make him stop, she cried. There was a kind of shame in that act, assuaging him with weakness. But she didn't know what else to do, and there was a shame in that too: she felt she should.

He swung his belt with one hand while his other hand held hers. His hand was thick and square, and held tight. Each lash of his belt propelled her forward and in that way they moved in a circle, their clasped hands the central pivot around which they turned.

The beatings took place at the foot of the stairs opposite the front door. Around and around they went in a space other people in other houses referred to as *the foyer*, until he wore himself out.

One day the beatings stopped. She didn't know why. And like him, she was never fully broken. Never fully whole.

Bad Dog

Mother was marching through the yard, shoulders back, chest thrust out, looking like a wind-up toy soldier, our escaped beagle loping out of her reach. We watched through the kitchen window, wondering if she would catch the silly dog that loved to bound out of the back door every chance he got. The set of her shoulders, the set of her face, she was going and going, and it was almost funny to see her rushing. Then she ran into a low branch of the plum tree. She fell straight to the ground. She lay there. Was she dead?

One of us ran to check.

One of us ran to the phone to call our father.

By the time he arrived home from work, she was at the kitchen sink, trying to remove the purplish stains on her blouse from the soft plums mashed into the grass under the tree.

She was angry about the stains. She was angry that she'd fallen. She was angry that the dog had escaped, an animal she'd never wanted to take care of. Most of all she was angry that our father had come home.

They had another fiery exchange in the kitchen, worse than the one they'd had earlier that morning before our father left for work.

It was unbearable to hear their words. We didn't really hear them. We heard the heat.

Our father stormed up the stairs. Something about the way he did it this time compelled one of us to follow him. The sound of the closet door in his bedroom opening and closing came down the hall.

The bedroom door was open. He sat at the foot of his bed, his eyes glazed over. A hunting rifle lay across his lap, like an oar, but he was not in a boat, though maybe he was intending to go somewhere.

After a time he replaced the gun to the closet and, passing the one of us standing in the doorway, left the house, presumably returned to work.

No one ever spoke of this day, the one of us never told about the rifle, but everyone agreed the beagle was bad, and the dog was given away.

Shredding

Dad stood up from the dinner table, one arm crooked behind his back as if he were concealing something from the rest of us. A small treat? Guess which hand. Mom's eyes focused on the page before her on the table, the latest murder mystery I'd carted home from the library for her. Dad might have waved what he held in his hand through the air, if he'd actually held something in his hand—tickets to paradise—but she wouldn't have noticed.

Dad winked at me like we were pals or something. His eyes behind the lenses of his glasses might have been mistaken for looking merry. He wanted me to do the dishes again, without protest. He thought he could charm me into starting.

My brother tipped his chair onto its back legs and whistled through his teeth. Wayne had become an exceptional whistler, while I was still unable to produce a note.

I looked down at the paper napkin in my lap. Lately my hands had taken to shredding paper. Earlier, I'd tried to flush pieces of my ripped-up notebook. The toilet overflowed and Dad demanded to know what I thought I was doing. I was always supposed to know what I was doing. *Think first*, Dad urged.

Not Mom. She wasn't expected to have a thought in her head, as if it were filled with a cloudless, thin atmosphere, devoid of color.

But she thought plenty. She had her demands: two weeks' worth of books, mysteries only, and no dawdling.

Dad stood by the stove, rubbing a wet sponge over the top, keeping me in his line of sight, ready with that pseudo-encouraging smile. I refused to look. The napkin grew flimsier in my hand.

Wayne's foot nudged mine under the table. This is what he did to say *Come on, don't make things worse.* Years ago, when Mom was well, supposedly, she'd told us that when I was a baby, Wayne had crawled out of his little bed each night and slept under my crib. He'd said we'd be married one day. Now he whistled and acted as if it were right that I had to do the work Mom wouldn't.

Under the table, the flimsy flimsy paper. My hands without thought. Bits of the napkin sifted to the floor like tiny clouds.

Someone would have to clean them up.

Celestial Bodies

As if in a game, my brother Derrick crawls across the plank he stretched from rooftop to rooftop.

Twelve stories down. How many feet equal one story? This is not the kind of math problem my teachers prepared me for.

And why? Why does he edge his body across the board—far enough out now that there is only the clotted shape of him like a hazy planet pasted on the night?

For Carlotta. A girl. One day I will understand the power of that, he tells me—of being a girl, I suppose he means, but I'm a girl who can't imagine a boy risking anything for me. I can't understand why I would want a boy to dare death for me.

What would I think of such a boy?

I imagine Carlotta over on her rooftop, a cigarette trailing from her hand as she lounges, cool. I glimpsed her one cloudy Saturday, eyes hidden behind her sunglasses, smiling at Derrick, adjusting the straps of her top.

"That body!" Derrick said.

He must be getting near: there is no sound of his progress anymore.

Only the traffic below, a sound I've imagined to be like the endless movement of the ocean. But at this moment, in this concentrated state of listening, I hear individual cars, stereo bass thumping, the diesel engine of a truck.

Picture the truck, picture the driver. The stupendous serendipity. The body crashing through. A heaven of shattering glass refracting light like glitter. Imagine no body ever knows what hit it.

A Lot to Learn

There she was, Amy Rodgers, over by the pool kissing my father. Our senior year party. She still wore her pink uniform from the Valley Dairy, her blonde hair sheeting down her back, the skirt too short. Very little yardage of fabric between where her hair ended and the hem of the skirt. My dad skulked in the shadows but I recognized him.

He had to know I was there.

The lamb-chop sideburns he'd grown this past month, were they raspy on Amy's face? Her perfect face. The corners of her mouth tilted upward as if she were privy to some amusing secret. When she and I cleared tables at work, pocketing tips that were never enough, Amy filled me in on all the details of her boyfriend Davey and his band, the roadies, groupies, everything I needed to learn.

Over in the shadows, Dad in his black t-shirt, the cut of his jeans wrong, slung too low on his hips, tight across the thighs. His arm wrapped around Amy's waist. I'd known enough not to wear my uniform, blemished with coffee stains and reeking of the grill. Did Amy's uniform smell? Was there a single blotch on it? More to the point, did Dad care?

Miles away Mom would be loaded down with her studies, cramming. I could picture her furrowed brow. Or facedown on her open textbook, snoring lightly, the way I'd come across her the last time I'd visited. She didn't have a boyfriend, and if she did, he would not be an employee of the Valley Dairy.

But Amy wasn't Dad's girlfriend, not by a long shot.

For a moment I tried to convince myself he was here at the party to check up on me. He was like an undercover agent, simply playing a role so he could do what he needed to do: learn all about me.

I turned to Ronnie Jarvis, grabbed him by the wrist, and pulled him to me. His eyebrows shot up in surprise. I pressed my lips over his, and eventually felt them give in, go pliant under mine. I felt his surprise transform into something else.

I had a lot to learn. I was going to.

A Depth so Familiar

The day after Christmas. Snowing. The countryside white. All the streets. Dark footprints led to the station. Inside, she watched the names of cities display as a train arrived or left. At the end of the day of her ninth birthday, wearing a paper crown on her head, she'd proclaimed she would never get married. Her little brothers and sisters slept upstairs, clutching dolls and stuffed animals, homework finished, candy stashed in their book bags. The roiling green along the edges of her life: that was memory. Mostly forgotten life. Once upon a time there were answering machines, and when she left a message she believed it played into an empty room. No one could have told her she would go with him because he had a scar. A depth so familiar. Anything can happen: anytime. The medallion he'd worn around his neck caught the sun through the window. His fingers locked around her arms. Anything can happen. She began to apologize, knowing it was too late. He said her voice reminded him of a naked corpse left on a tower for vultures. A smell of sulphur, hot metal, ionizing clouds. Her lip plump with blood. She tried and failed to recall every word she'd said. She tried to seal herself away from the touch of his hand on her body. Days from now the row of purple fingerprints stamped into her arm. Open that door and I'll forget, he'd said. But she left. She'd gotten this far, to the station. Trains arrived and left again, and would. Snow would fall, melt, fall again.

The Girl and the Stone

The stone was green. It may have been moss that made it so. He didn't know; he picked the stone up from the side of the road and threw it.

Ahead of him the girl fell when the rock hit her. She went down.

She lay with her eyes closed, mud on her cheek and in her hair.

He nudged her foot with his boot. She didn't move. He pushed her onto her side with his black boot.

Now he saw the back of her head. The red blood.

He picked up her pale hand. "Get up," he said. "Get up now."

A wren alit on a branch overhead and sang. It swept its gaze back and forth and sang, its breast pumping.

The girl did not stir. Dark clouds moved in. Far off a dog barked.

The wind lifted her plaid skirt.

She must be cold on the damp ground.

Her red blood burned bright in his mind's eye as he ran for home. The brilliance did fade as the years passed.

Imprint

I lived in a large house beside a lake, filled with massive furniture, polished floors, stuffed bookshelves. A huge mirror covered the foyer wall. I never looked in the glass when I stood before it: my eyes examined the gilded frame with its intricately carved heads of cherubs.

My father often called me into his study to force me out of my delusions and into the real world. Hunched over his desk, he could tell that I stood waiting, but he spoke only when he was good and ready. I longed to escape upstairs to my room where a model airplane kit always awaited me.

I never knew what my delusion was but it seemed to have to do with my father's estranged wife, whom I vaguely remembered as a quiet, thin woman with immense sad eyes and a tiny pucker of a mouth, dressed in dark turtleneck sweaters. The delusion seemed to have to do with how my father had believed that he was providing me with a mother—my own had died shortly after my birth—and how his plan hadn't worked out.

The woman who came in to do the laundry sometimes alluded to my father's sorrow while she ironed his starched shirts. She would sigh and plunk the iron down onto the ironing board and smooth her hand across the white cloth as if she were caressing the face of a loved one. She had no idea of what went on in that study.

I began going in secret with a classmate to the Catholic Church and to catechism classes. The priest, who treated us with patience and kindness, would place his palms on my head. His warm and damp hands left an imprint on my forehead that would last me a time.

Sometimes I wanted to be him. I wanted to have such a class.

That did not happen.

I acquired a wife of my own. She blessed the scars on my wrists with her kisses. She spoke in tones of gold and mercy.

Where is the dictionary, the field guide on intimate behavior?

My words would come out of the dark night sky, and I waited to see if they would make my wife bleed. Something rose in my chest as I felt my hands on her, and I would relent only after she made eye contact. Glassy-eyed, she no doubt wished my size were hers. I took one of her hands inside mine and squeezed until she fell to the floor in pain, lay still as a sleeping bird. The satisfying snap of the collapse of her spirit.

That was fifty years ago, and at least as many letters of questions from me to her. But the last ten or so have brought no replies. I may have outlived her as I have outlived others who made up my life. That is how I explain it, the silence, that I'm left breathing. I'm uncertain of any meaning.

Weather of the World

When I was young I liked to lie under the apple tree and think about the weather across the world, just beyond the setting sun. I imagined in charge a grandmotherly person with translucent skin, pale as rice paper, who ate orchids and wanted a kind word from the eldest son. Pools of pure feeling filled me.

Then I learned that I wasn't the eldest. I wouldn't be an heir. I had a half-brother somewhere in Albany, New York, an adult with his own life, whom my father had had dinner with one recent evening.

My mother revealed this in the family room, with its oppressing walls of glass shelves that held the rocks, the coins, the blown glass figurines. I saw how my mother had been simply another addition to his collections. For that, what had she willingly given up?

Cracks in the stories of his whereabouts were showing. I wanted her to tell me what sacrifice she had made but she said, *No! Will you listen?*

I couldn't; I'd heard enough; I'd thought I had.

Then one night she called me into the same room and told me that he'd been found by a river upstate. Fifteen stab wounds, one to the neck, but it was the blunt jab with an oar that had killed him.

What haunting and uncertain conditions had led to this, I was still too unformed to speculate.

I fled. To the archway that led into a maze of narrow alleys forming the heart of town.

In the darkness the sound of a child's voice came, stolen through a thin-paned window. Odors of rotting vegetation. Distant footsteps sounded, faded. The humidity pressed against my bare arms like a second skin.

The sky split and fat raindrops fell.

I turned my feet to home.

There, I fell asleep in a neat surrender, a dangerous and safe position. Where I remained for many years, my eyes dry as dead leaves. The apple tree aged, lost branches. One winter storm finished it off. I began to awaken.

Woman in a Dark Gray Dress

Two voices that have run like rails through his life, parallel and disconnected, converge and intertwine. Now is his only chance. To stop the desperate dreams. He'll soothe her, run his hand over her arm. As if feeling for the wound. The elevator doors slide open. The smell of snow. As if on the side of Mont Blanc. A monstrous violet orchid towers. An old record player stands in front of the couch. She in the dark gray dress stilled on the brocade sofa. She doesn't look up. No, it's too much for him to expect of himself. In his pocket the well-chosen card. His fingers trace words etched into thick white paper. The silence becomes more like a sound in the bed. The bed that serves as a cage.

An Arrangement

Each day on the way home from school she walked by a dark and deteriorating building. The faded letters on the weathered sign hanging over the door, that looked as if it might fall and maim an innocent passerby someday, said *Jake's Tavern,* if one put a little imagination into the reading. Men, smelling of whiskey, old sweat and dead fish, idled inside, while she moved from class to class, science, math, social studies. Always drawn to what she didn't know, she longed to enter the tavern, just to see.

You're never satisfied, her mother often said. She wished for a mother who would patiently plait her long hair into a braid, asking what she wanted to be when she grew up. But her mother insisted her hair be kept short, manageable. It never seemed to occur to her mother that one day she would be old enough to leave home and would have to do something.

When the time came and she moved out, she meandered from one job to another, one school to another, one man to another. No different from any girl who hadn't been worth the time spent to comb her pretty hair.

Hair changes over time, thins, loses color.

An aging woman, she returned to the town to visit her ancient mother in her sick bed. Regret etched into the lines that crossed the woman's face, while she sat and held the dry hand until the woman fell asleep.

She took a walk uptown, discovered the tavern had been torn down. In its place stood a florist's shop, vases of gaudy blooms crowding the window front. There was nothing for it but to buy an arrangement. To feel something goodly and important when her mother opened her eyes to the bright blossoms and smiled.

Fragmentation

She hated the story about how the old fisherman cut up the sea stars, throwing each arm into the sea—an abundance of mutilated creatures, five fragments then for every one—it frightened her to think about an ocean of broken living beings awash in their own weeping juices, working to recreate themselves, vulnerable and having to hide until they could become whole again; her eyes were red-rimmed in the mirror when she gave up trying to sleep and went into the bathroom for a cool drink of water to rinse away the salt.

A Worn Sock

A hole had opened in Josie's sock under the pad of her foot not too far from her pinky toe. It didn't bother her. She wasn't like her husband Carl, who, as a boy, couldn't bear if the seams of his socks didn't lay in a clean horizontal line across the top of his foot, or if extra material bunched up over his heels once he'd stepped into his oxfords. Carl had planned to do something about how inexact sock measurements were when he grew up, his mother once confided to Josie. The two of them had been sitting outside The Coffeeshop having *afternoon tea*, a term Carl's mother used metaphorically, as she herself was on her second glass of chardonnay at three p.m. Her eyes were moist with merriment. Ah, Carl. Her first-born, such a pistol.

The memory of this tête-à-tête came to Josie as she pushed her foot with the worn sock and its hole into her hiking boot. Seven months of marriage and Carl was more of an enigma than ever. Where was he now? He might be at his studio downtown where he constructed odd, elaborate sculptures using precisely folded paper he dared anyone to label origami. A night person, Carl often left their bed after she'd gone to sleep. She imagined him driving through the drowsing neighborhood, a sliver of moon witness when he let himself into the warehouse on Canal Street. It was dangerous to go there alone, but he only widened his eyes at her when she said that and told her that it turned him on when she made proclamations.

Josie laced her boot and sat quietly on the edge of the bed. Outside the window, a squirrel jumped to a higher branch and scolded a creature she couldn't see. She could wait for Carl to show, which would be a mistake—it could be tomorrow when she heard from him—or she could head out to the trail alone on this perfect Sunday.

She stood, her knees unhinging stiffly. She ignored the movement in the mirror across the room—her reflection that she knew would disappoint her—and crossed the room and began to feel the hole. The tacky spot where the flesh of her foot made contact with the inside of her boot made itself increasingly known as she went out the door. The sensation would either worsen as she went or she would grow numb to it. She didn't want to stop to change.

I Should Let You Go

She phoned him at work just because, no real reason. It had simply occurred to her to give him a call like they used to do when they were new. To hear your voice, they'd say by way of explanation. The kitchen, early morning, was sunny, and lightened her spirits; she'd woken up in a mood, something wrong but nothing really. They had no real problems.

She dialed and poured a glass of water and stood waiting for him to answer, looking out the window at the tender magnolia blooms close to the glass, the sky behind so blue it could crack. February already.

He answered, his voice sounding rushed and, when he heard that nothing was wrong, quizzical. He answered her questions. Yes, his morning was going fine, busy, too busy, he was glad she called. The searching tone infected his voice.

She said again, No real reason. Her eyes returned to the magnolia, a lump forming in her throat.

He gave a short laugh, evidently talking to someone nearby, and she said she should let him go, and he said, no, no, he was just walking over to the café for another cup of coffee to put down his gullet.

She wished they talked more kindly about themselves. *To put down my gullet* was an expression that had come from her mother. *Get some food down your gullet.*

Harsh, he agreed. She swallowed. She said she supposed there was some love in the words, as in reverse psychology. She tried to tease out the idea as she talked, and he laughed a little louder.

She could try to explain that her mother wasn't able to show softness, not even in her language, that her mother didn't want anyone to know how much she cared. It seemed that this could be true; she wanted it to be.

His voice was loud, asking, What did you say, hello? Are you still there? When we met I thought, he said, lowering his voice, she is the biggest small person in the world. You walk into the room and fill it up.

This was catching love in words, a kind of contagion, because she wanted to believe what he believed, and knew it could grow and, if they were lucky, not like a sickness. She could go on with this thinking, her throat aching, or they could say goodbye. For now. She stretched herself tall in the kitchen with its high vaulted ceiling, filling her body with breath, and turned away from the window.

The Girl in the Picture

In the photo my daughter poses, smiling, dark hair sleek as the coat of a young filly. On the chipped cement steps, the tips of the black leather boots she loved peek from under a lacy hem. Beside the stairs, dirt redder than rust. One of the last years we lived together; she was sixteen; she couldn't wait to leave the South.

This is what familiarity demands: that I examine every detail again as if new clues will present themselves.

In our apartment she liked to lie on the rug in my room to talk after school. I lay on the bed and listened. *We all mock the silly, the stupid, the garish*, she said, *but why?* She stared into my face like she saw something new there to examine. Sometimes I might have an answer for her piquant questions. Sometimes she would respond, *Old woman, surely you jest*. We would never be alone again in that way.

She was always looking deep into my face.

When she was four, just before I left her father, she said, *If he didn't mean it he should say he's sorry*. I knew he would never apologize and an apology would never alter the course we were following. The rest of her life he would have a way of loving her before walking out again and vanishing for years.

When she was seven and we played a card game of War she said, *Why does the king always win over the queen? Who made up the rules?*

At fourteen she was always giving her stuff away, like the expensive leather jacket I could barely afford that she gifted a runaway boy. *So many people seem concerned with the wrong things*, she said.

Once not long before the picture was taken, she said she was sorry that she wanted so much. We were in the gourmet market where she'd loaded our cart with mangoes, a coconut, chocolate macaroons. I hope I said the right thing.

In the photo a wing of her hair lifts in the breeze and casts a shadow over the side of her face. The next moment, after the shutter clicked, her hair would have dropped back into place. There must be something yet for me to discover by looking.

Though it's cold this time of year in Midville, I sit on the balcony waiting until the sun clears the tops of the tallest pines. I never wanted to live here either. Girl in the picture, you certainly didn't make it easy on me. She would say *Was I supposed to?*

Human Movement

The coldest summer in forty-odd years, earthquakes in places there'd never been, and her mother dying in a hospital bed across the country. She bought plane tickets. He went to fill up the car. She waited by the curb for him to drive up and take them to the airport. Waxy juniper shrubs set in tired gray bark chips lined the sidewalk. Something about the bushes. They could sense lost causes. The car was waiting now, the impatient engine exciting the air, warming her legs. What would it be to get in and simply ride hour after hour, no destination?

They arrived in the middle of the night at the house of her sister who lived near the hospital. No one was awake, but on the phone earlier her sister had directed her to take the room with the unmarked black door just at the head of the stairs.

Inside smelled vaguely of cedar and cinnamon. On the bureau top rested a matchbook with an image of pineapple on it above the name of an inn in Costa Rica. Next to the matches, an ancient volume of Mother Goose.

She knew she should sleep before it was time to see her mother. But she found an eyelash on her pillow and sleep felt impossible. She sat in the chair by the window, listening for snores, for any sounds that might mark the whereabouts of the others in the house. He stretched out across the top of the covers and propped his head on his hand. Let's take a shower, he suggested, and because she ultimately could find no real objection, she agreed.

Divided, they didn't understand the rules that kept them separate. It was something to do with the swirling waters of the world of the dead. *Of the dying,* he said. Steam rose and water slid down their bodies.

She stepped out from the shower onto the gold-rimmed mat, where he waited holding out a towel. Droplets of water clung to the hair on his chest above the towel wound around his waist. He made appreciative noises in his throat as he eyed her nakedness.

She avoided looking at his face to see what expression would win there. She didn't want to share her body. She had shared enough of it already. Her words seemed high-strung. Age had withered her wit, wasn't that it?

He stepped away from her and finished drying himself. Light began to crack through the gap under the window blind. She raised the blind and saw a large bird leave the limb of the tree beside the glass, no doubt startled by her human movement.

The bird, species unknown, flapped his leathery-looking wings, perhaps in a panic, before it dropped. She opened the window and looked out.

At the sound she released he rushed to her side.

They stood, heads out the window, looking down at the patio bricks where the fallen bird lay still. They didn't speak of what would happen next.

Packet of Tea

She keeps a special packet containing a ginger teabag tucked away next to her jewelry box on her dresser, a packet she'd finally removed from her purse in order to see it less often. Her daughter B. gave the tea to her the last time they met, unplanned. What may turn out to be the last time she will ever see her girl.

Her feelings for her daughter B., especially when B. was a child, were so intense that she sometimes mistook them for pain. She'd feared that she wouldn't survive seeing calamity overtake B. Still, though B. herself had been the biggest surprise, she'd also known life was certain to spring many more.

B. struggled as a young woman, going from one college to another before finally dropping out, hopping from job to job, from marriage to marriage. She tried not to despair as she helped her daughter through her troubles. The time came when once again B. was unemployed, broke, and divorcing, and she decided that her daughter would have to make her own way. B. said that she misunderstood her; she had always misunderstood who she was.

Then B. showed up unexpectedly in the cafeteria of the hospital, where up on the seventh floor, her own mother was dying. B. handed her the packet of tea with a look of love in her face, a gleam of pride. How dear was B.'s every penny at that point. It hurt to know that her daughter had unnecessarily spent money to comfort her. And on such expensive tea! A standard tea bag would have done.

Yet she was touched. When she thanked B., their embrace was nonetheless stiff, unyielding. B. needed to learn to take charge of her own life. Her dying mother had taught her that. B. left the cafeteria, her beautiful head held high.

The packet with its dull green color is the first item her eyes fall on when she enters her bedroom. This is because the woman she hires to clean her house moves the tea from its usual place out of sight when she dusts the dresser top.

She tries to tell herself that there is no use to think in the same breath of B.'s financial difficulties and her ability to pay the cleaning woman to do what she could do herself. She refuses the cleaning woman's message to put the packet where it belongs. Where would that be?

More Apart, More Alive

The only entrance a ramp that runs alongside the building. A two-story structure: concrete, cement, glass. Blue Volvo station wagon parked in front. They enter together, alone in dulled dreams. Merely another couple. Photographs in the office clustered on a desktop. Under the warmth of a lamp. She asks who is who and admires the professional's sunny family. The talk of unhappiness commences. No distractions now, the couple hears one another. They've paid for the privilege. Ragged, torn, tattered their story, more apart, more alive. The presence of an unfamiliar woman's spirit is raised in her. A great dark cloud, thrum of bees in a hive. When they arrive home she can't enter the house. The first star shows over the roof. Temperature cooling. Palms sting, wooden handle of the old-fashioned spade. The freshly turned dirt of her mother's prized flower garden. Sound of the door closing in the dark, silhouette of his approaching figure. He climbs onto the rock, king of the mountain. She'll tell him everything, won't she. Until no trace of the old strangeness remains.

Cherished

Dressing to go to dinner at the Schaffers', Douglas pulled on the pair of socks his ex-lover had knitted for him. There was a little hole in one, where his big toe showed. The Schaffers lived down the street, the middle house on the cul-de-sac, in an Eichler restored to its original condition, and they expected guests to remove their shoes upon entering. Douglas' thick socks would draw attention for their colorful pattern—and for the opening that showed the naked flesh of his toe.

Shoeless at the Schaffers', as he'd expected, the eyes of the other guests were drawn to the hole, but they spoke only instead about the green, blue, and magenta yarn. He liked thinking about who would eventually acknowledge the obvious imperfection. That person would be his new friend. He could use one. Since Miranda had left his life, an open place in the weave of his days needed filling.

Douglas pictured Miranda sitting under the halo of the lamplight, logs crackling behind her in the fireplace, sweat collecting on her upper lip. It was never cold enough for a fire, but it was something she cherished, an idea of home, of domesticity, and he willingly went bare-chested and wore shorts to accommodate her illusion.

Miranda's steel needles flashing in the light. Sometimes she faced a problem in her handicraft that confounded her, but he'd assumed that she'd always overcome the trouble. It was a complete surprise to learn differently, to find the stitches give way in his sock, the shock of his toe emerging in unwanted freedom.

He would love these socks until the day he died. He sat in his shirt and his trousers in the Schaffers' living room and waited for his new friend to speak.

U+2204

Katrina found a brown fedora lying in the aisle of the market, which she'd entered to escape the rain. She cruised around the store, pretending to look at items on the shelves—miniature boxes of cereal, paper plates, packages of gummy candies—waiting to see if anyone would claim the hat.

The store emptied of its last two customers. The fedora was meant for her, wasn't it, and she purchased an overpriced box of colored chalk with her last three dollars.

Outside, she pulled the hat low over her brow. Within a few blocks her sweater was soaked, her black tights clung to her thighs, and her sneakers were drenched, and she was shivering. But her face was dry. Up ahead, the bus shelter.

A sort of glow emanated from it, haloing the people inside who huddled into themselves like separate islands. No one made eye contact as she approached. At the last minute she made her decision and turned into the shelter. She took a seat on the bench in the corner.

Next to her, hood pulled over his head so that she could see only the tip of his pointed nose, a guy hunched over a deck of cards he shuffled in his hands. Katrina watched from the corner of her eye. He did something elaborate with the deck. He was a casino dealer, or an aspiring magician. He began to rock on the bench while he slid the cards back and forth between his hands.

Soon Katrina realized that this wasn't a normal deck. Instead of hearts and clubs and spades and diamonds, the cards depicted unusual characters. Mathematical perhaps. She'd taken a logics course once and thought she recognized a symbol.

The guy paused, his hands moving to conceal the cards. Where'd you get that hat, he asked. I lost one just like it.

"My uncle gave it to me for my birthday just before he shipped off to Afghanistan, where he'd died within the month," she said.

Uncle Roger, he said.

Katrina said, "Yeah."

He sent me these cards from over there, his best deck, the guy said. A generous man.

Katrina agreed, "So giving." The bus pulled up and hissed and the others boarded, and Katrina and the guy watched the bus pull away, a wall of water splashing high but stopping short of reaching them in the shelter.

How Things Are

"Is everything okay?"
     "It's fine."
     "It's fine?"
     "It's okay."

My Descent

On the brink. Feet sliding before me. Jewel tone sky above achingly bright, but I'm not looking. My eyes are on this path, which is probably not a path at all, is merely a trailing vestige from some unknown other's passing. My choir teacher said something about moving down the scale, I remember the metronome ticking in the background, but I was thirteen then and hadn't felt inclined to ask what he meant. He had a thick gray mustache, Mr. Kemp, and surely he had been young once, had gone to the movies, taking a girl for whom he bought a large tub of popcorn with extra butter, in those days never considering the effect of the fat on their arteries. Truth is, if it had been real butter, no issue. But likely it was not, likely it was margarine, or as my mother would have said, *oleo*. A word that sounds like a yodel, you can imagine a Swiss miss calling across the slopes, *oleo, oleo*. A musical voice. To grab Mr. Kemp's attention. He would ask her to shape her lips in various ways over her teeth, to produce sounds long and short, long and short, and her skirt short, short. Stop, I'm thinking. Break it up. Heidi's red skirt, her long pale legs. She's hearty, robust. This mountainside, sun brilliant on the snow, hard and crisp, stabbing my eyes. I'm going down. Patch sewn on the left breast pocket of my parka, a rainbow, hand-embroidered by someone in Tibet. A fair trade purchase. The artisan will live much better for many more years of creating her richly-hued emblems to stitch onto our clothing. Clothing that will not save us. Facsimiles of scientific phenomena sutured to cloth, carried to the grave, to tell someone a tale. I'm going down, Heidi here in my heart, the Tibetan's care radiating from over it like a flag. Girls who are with me for no reason that I can say. And without the understanding, perhaps I am alone. You will say I was alone.

The Associate

Her husband told her he was going out of the country the second week of the month, just after her birthday. A strange sensation crept over her skin, and she felt such as when the person you are trying to reach is sitting with his phone, unanswering. That evening they had dinner at the apartment of his associate who had invited them, he explained, because she, being new to the city, was lonely. She wanted them to feel comfortable with her. She needed friends.

Her place smelled of curries and something vaguely like decaying sunflowers. The woman's face reminded her of a finely cracked mirror but not one so broken that you would discard it. Possibly, the associate was not her husband's lover after all. The woman showed them into the living room, where they were to wait the ten or fifteen minutes until dinner, the wine they brought left unopened on the table.

They were alone in the small room and quiet, some unseen threads connecting them to the earlier conversation. *You are supposed to talk,* she said, because she needed to learn his secret. He placed his finger to his mouth and shook his head.

The meal was dry, and a large cockatiel squawked in its cage as they ate, rustling its dusty feathers, powdery motes flailing in the fading sunlight. After, they waited in the hall for the elevator, white light illuminating the number of their floor, then disappearing, and the doors never sliding open.

They descended the three flights of stairs to the street and began the long walk back across the bridge. Birds hunted underneath, sending up a cacophony of muted noises.

He stopped to look out over the river low against its banks. He always liked to look at water, no matter its qualities, and true to his nature, he seemed to see the river as it might have been once, a rush of water over the huge rocks, alive, pushing to the sea. He took her arm, placing his hand between her armpit and breast, and she said nothing, thinking of a time when their bodies seemed so uncomplicated, so vital, so known.

Nora and Paul at The Coffeeshop

"The usual?" the barista asked Paul. She smiled at him and tucked her dark hair behind her ear, pierced and decorated with a length of glittering studs.

Nora wasn't sure she'd heard correctly—*the usual?* Paul's flushing face confirmed that was right. He refused to meet Nora's eyes and fumbled at his pocket for his wallet.

"I'll get us a seat," Nora said and found them a booth in the back, far from the counter.

She sat and brushed grains of sugar off the table. She pictured the girl's face again, how it had brightened when she'd seen Paul. When had he found time to come here—where would he have told Nora he was going? She searched her mind, went backwards through the days since The Coffeeshop had opened at the end of their street. How delighted they'd been then. They would walk up together mornings, they'd said. Lunch sometimes: the café offered exactly the right menu. So far, they'd been, before today, only once. Together. Now it was evident Paul had been sneaking up here himself all along.

Where was he? Beside Nora two noisy children, a girl and a boy, slipped out of their booth and began chasing one another up the aisle. Nora looked over at their mother, who was deep in conversation on her cell phone. Nora trained her eyes on the woman, who surely must feel the weight of her attention. The mother seemed to studiously avoid looking Nora's way. It was a problem of some sort. Nora was becoming invisible. The woman tapped a dark plastic stirrer on the tabletop in front of her to emphasize something she was saying.

Paul approached, carrying a tray with two coffee mugs and a small plate of pastries. Wisps of steam hovered over the white cups.

And here was the little girl running and screeching, not looking, straight into Paul's legs.

He tried to recover the tray—it was obvious how he did. But too late. It all happened in a moment but that stretched on agonizingly long. The hot coffee pouring over the child, her face, the screaming, Paul going down, mugs cracking on the stone tile, the little boy standing stock still in the aisle.

"What have you done?" screamed the mother. "My God! What?" She struggled to move out of the booth. But her eyes were on Nora. She had addressed Nora.

Magpies

He had an older sister whose face reminded Lydia of a magpie in the TV cartoons of her childhood. Now that Lydia thought of it, she realized that the cartoon had featured two birds, twins. How fitting. He had been enmeshed with his sister in a way just this side of pathological. The family pushed the myth—he'd insisted it was a myth—of the two siblings as practically twins. They were that close, the mother liked to croon.

Lydia had seen photographs of the two in Halloween costumes, dressed up as Raggedy Ann and Andy. How humiliating to have to have been Raggedy Andy. Lydia tried to discern something behind the lipstick-enhanced red smile in the boy in the photos.

The sister's appearance costumed as Raggedy Ann was an improvement. She actually looked like a little girl you could love.

He typically exited the room when the mother brought out the pictures. Once he'd charged out of the house and stepped in dog shit in the backyard, and was quite angry with everyone later, when he returned inside.

When Lydia had first met the sister, she was unprepared for the woman's appearance—the sharp nose and thin lips. The mother had always referred to her daughter as a "pixie," and he'd always smiled fondly. Lydia had been prepared to love the sister. The woman's harsh features turned out to be her softest rebuke.

Now Lydia listened to him speak on the phone to his sister. As usual, he slipped in occasional words of comfort. Evidently the sister was in one of her typical modes of operation, venting a litany of problems. Once he'd put his sister on speakerphone and parodied her as she blathered. Which might have made Lydia choke with laughter if she hadn't been so repulsed by the nattering voice and by his inability to hang up.

Lydia looked up the quote on the Internet first to be sure, then copied it down on a little pad and set it before him: "We exaggerate misfortune and happiness alike. We are never as bad off or as happy as we say we are. Honore de Balzac." He glanced at the words, gave Lydia a frown, and turned away.

Lydia felt her face flush. So that's how he wanted to play it! Her fingers trembled as she returned to the Internet, her favorite homewares website, where she entered into the search field "sheets." She looked for sets with the highest thread counts. She'd get the ones she wanted this time. Screw cost!

Oh, what am I doing? she thought. She pushed the laptop away and went to the kitchen for a glass of water.

She heard him from the other room, despite his lowered voice, say, "Shut up, shut up, shut up." A tortured whisper. It sounded like he was crying. Then the small click, like he'd hung up. Silence extended.

Lydia waited, waited for him to call her to him. She sipped the cool water, and watched out the kitchen window a tiny gray bird hop across the porch, its slow progress across the wide floorboards. It could fly if it wanted.

A Weak Light Shining through the High Small Window

After months of rehab her husband's homecoming was set for the following week. The doctors said that he might recover more but that no one knows all there is to know about injuries to that specific part of the brain. Soon her husband would join her in the hospital's support group that she'd been attending, a group comprised of caretakers and patients, a rotating cast of facilitators, nurses, holy people of one ilk or another.

She had no idea what he would make of the group but felt apprehensive thinking about it this morning on her way to the meeting. A storm emerged from nowhere. Gusts of wind blew the sudden rain sideways and sent people running from their cars to the hospital doors. In the eerie air pressure she felt a kind of weightlessness but without the pleasure. Perhaps she was growing ill.

Despite the rogue weather, the group attendance was robust. She spotted two newcomers: an older woman with a mustache who perched in her wheelchair as if it were a throne and her grim-faced Latino attendant with extraordinary, long fingernails polished fire engine red. A young man maneuvered his wheelchair to create concentric patterns in the dust on the floor, intensely focused on his activity. The floor was always dusty.

Folding tables lining one side of the room held a row of duplicate white busts of Lincoln, perhaps a therapeutic art project. Five computers occupied the tables on the opposite wall, their screens oscillating softly. A man in a ski cap, ambulatory but badly listing to one side, approached and began asking her questions in rapid fire: Have you had oysters? Is an espresso really worth a blouse? Do the boys like your brother?

The last question bothered her for some reason. She had only a sister. But, she realized, now she would live with her husband as if he were her brother.

She found a vacant corner to stand in. Nearby a pair of women—unexpected caretakers like her—discussed their houses in worried tones. At home she'd already had completed the necessary modifications: ramps, easily navigable passageways, the master bedroom converted into a space of storage for all of her husband's equipment.

A feverish flush surged through her with the memory that arose, her husband sitting at her side in their room the time she'd taken ill, his cool palm on her forehead. He stood decisively and declared they were going to the ER. She'd had an emergency appendectomy. He may have saved her life, the surgeon said. She wondered if her husband would ever remember a time when he'd cared for her, a time when he was able to.

The facilitator started the meeting, a weak light shining now through the high small window behind him. She'd seen him here before and surmised he was a recovered patient. Slouching terribly, he wore an ill-fitting blue blazer. His speech reached a point of apogee, his arms spread wide. *Don't limit yourself,* he said. *Reach. Grab what you can.*

The man who'd blasted her with questions twitched in his chair and repeated the words back softly. People weren't to interrupt, but this rule was rarely enforced. The man's voice rose as he repeated the words. A young woman in her early twenties with scars running down the side of her face, seeming more bored than angry, waved her hand in the air. From her plastic chair, she told the man to sit. *Be quiet!* But he merely turned to her and continued repeating, *grab what you can*. The facilitator stood helpless.

It was impossible to think about bringing her husband here. She went up to his floor, skipping the elevator, taking the eight flights of stairs. When she neared his room, she heard him telling his favorite nurse how beautiful she was. The nurse exited the room and, pink-faced, gave her a wry smile when she noticed her in the corridor.

On his tray, a bowl contained buckwheat kasha with milk that he splashed his spoon in aimlessly with his good hand. His dark hair was still damp. Each morning he wet his hair at the sink with his palm, another new habit.

He seemed agitated. Perhaps he was worried about how they would manage together at home. She wasn't sure what home meant to him. He supposedly still had no memory of the accident. She herself had waked out of nightmares several times at the imagined blast of the truck's horn on the freeway.

She ran her hand over his pale arm to soothe him. Before the accident she'd constantly, effusively told him how much she loved him. All the while she was falling in love with another man, a man she would never see again—that was finished. She didn't know if her husband had suspected.

She stroked the softened flesh of his wrist. Would he ever come to remember the woman who'd been in the car with him that night? And what would happen if so—would he then have to grieve the loss of her? What was grief to him? Would he experience emotional pain?

He put the spoon down on the tray and looked at her, his eyes shining from within his affectless face, waiting. *Grab what you can*, the facilitator had urged. Oh, wasn't that a pretty plan! She tucked her chin against his shoulder, and breathed in the scent of healing flesh, of hospital soap, of all that had come between them.

Marvelous Gardener Tends to the Sapling

No other feeling so slowly and uncomfortably crawls over a body like defeat. Slow and deliberate, it's masculine. Though she'd tried, she couldn't manage the grounds of her new home. She called the number in the ad in the paper. The gardener said, *No one goes it alone anymore, ever.* He arrived first thing the next day.

His face was sharp, as if cut from a knife, but his eyes were deep and luminous and kind as he greeted her, tipping his hat, a black feather tucked into the band of the straw fedora. She leaned forward over the doorstep to take his hand. The crevices of his fingers were clean. Flesh warm.

He smiled, and simultaneously the fog shifted, and her shadow appeared on the porch slate. It was as though layers of his body had become apparent, stratified, composed of the collision and attraction of molecules. A marvelous stranger sent by a god. She simultaneously felt she was in the presence of someone unknowable and someone she'd known for ages, before memory.

As a younger woman she had felt that love was no big mystery. It was simply admiration mixed with an impulse to settle down. That understanding had made her feel that life afforded some control, she saw that now. The idea had never borne out.

She showed him the property, pointing out the fruit tree that she couldn't identify—persimmon or quince, she suggested. He measured her with his eyes. He surveyed the grounds as if they were his. All this pleased her though once she wouldn't have stood for it. A spell gripped her that she was likely to break if she looked too closely.

He named plants and shrubs, said what they needed, outlined his plans. He unloaded his simple tools from the truck and began at the top of the hill. Two downhill paths stood out on the uneven rise, one long and meandering, one short and steep.

She found a private spot near the house to sit where she could watch him work, his form small and dark against the bleached sunlight.

He unearthed a sapling that needed to be moved, tender green in the increasing light. Cradling the dead weight of the young tree as if it were his only child, he turned to give her a look—she thought, his features indiscernible from where she sat. Yet, something passed between them in the still moment.

She shook herself. Rose and dusted the back of her pants, bits of sharp leaves and twig debris rough under her hands.

Inside the house she stood before the open kitchen cupboard, looking at, but not seeing, a half-filled shelf of goods she couldn't remember buying. She looked a long time. Time was passing. She could be as good as the gardener. The thing was to begin, to make the selection as if it mattered.

Two Is the Only Number

Human kind cannot bear very much reality –T.S. Eliot

In the evenings my heartbeats quicken: an indication of stress, of fear. At such times I want to remember safe places. I want to remember his room, walls the blue of a glacial lake, the small jeweled ornaments that hung from the ceiling light, the bed pillows that rustled with feathers. To reach the other side of the island where he lived I had to fly and so we almost never saw each other. But then I was undaunted by difficult odds. I didn't want to just drift away. I didn't want my love to burn to ashes like my mother's had. I paid a pilot to take me and sat looking out the window at the Grecian flat earth below, the encircling water sparkling. On the far shore, when the faint line running down the brown-green surface appeared, we landed. When my lover opened the door that last time, the one time I like most of all to remember, he spoke immediately, a small glimpse of his restless soul. Two is the only number that's ever made me feel complete, he said. He asked that I be his. He bathed my head with perfumed water, stroked my crown with tenderness. On my finger he placed an old ring with a sliver of milky stone in the setting. Our vows burned white against our skin. What was it like to occupy my body at that moment? So many years ago. So many heartbeats. Is it mind or body that prevents the merge of time present, time past? My heart continues its beat while light filters out, darkness settles in.

Inscription of Time

She began to lose family members. Very soon only her friends remained, her contemporaries. But this was the natural order. It was folded into the wind. Then two of her beloved friends fell ill and were gone quickly. One morning, her tired heart prompted the thought that there was no reason to arise from bed.

But a call came from an old lover, who wanted her to visit him at his apartment on the West Side. Years ago, after they'd gone their separate ways, he'd been in a car accident at the track—he'd been a high-ranked driver on the circuit—and remained in a coma for weeks until, miraculously, he'd recuperated. She'd heard about this through another person, one of the beloved friends now gone.

His block building was grimy white, surrounded by concrete, and a wire shopping cart with a bent wheel waited by the entrance. Inside, the elevator shook as it rose the three floors. A large fern, alive and green, stood beside his door.

She knocked and his keys jingled in the lock. He opened the door, a black beanie pulled low to his eyes. As equally uncharacteristic as the hat were his grandiose button-up shirt top-stitched with golden thread and the ruffling white scarf wound around his neck. What stunned her most, however, was the sadness. She'd known others like this on whom sadness was refined and elegant, but they'd always been strangers.

One large room comprised his apartment, scented like verbena extract. Yet the smell barely overlaid that of old age. She sat on the lumpy sofa, her eyes drawn to the scars on his hands clutching the arms of his chair, live remainders of the neat stitches that had pieced those hands back together. His entire body had been fitted into a whole with a mixture of plastic and metal parts, components that might live longer than he. Where did such materials go when the flesh was gone?

Once he'd said that he never wanted to live beyond the point where his body was not his own. He didn't want to become *defective*, that was his word.

He talked in a thin voice, occasionally turning to stare at the door. Each time that she followed his eyes along that path the light in the doorway appeared different, the blue shade of the painted wood shifted. He spoke of frequently hearing his mother's voice, of her conversations with the angels.

A dark form edged against the ceiling, an unattached shadow.

Daylight drained away.

She stayed on, listening. This was the only thing she could do to save his life, she thought.

Next door, a woman shouted angrily about the TV remote. Words from the show came through the wall: *I'm not living with you. We occupy the same cage.*

A smile creased his scarred face. *Tennessee Williams*, he said. *There's no retribution for rudeness*, he said. He sighed and brushed invisible crumbs from his lap. *I must be kind to the I that I once was.*

He stood creakily and went to his bookshelf and pulled out an old album of polaroids. He removed a photo from beneath its plastic sheath and handed it to her, an inscription of time and place etched in blue ballpoint ink below the image of his racecar.

She squinted to make it out. A tiny helmeted head inside the car. Her mind with its human need completed the pattern, decided: yes, that was him, the little circular dot in the picture.

He took her gently by the arm and led her to the door, and asked her not to return.

It was as if he'd understood what she hadn't known until that moment. That she needed an ending.

The ending wasn't one she'd wanted. But maybe one day when she slid the photo from her bag, it would be different.

ACKNOWLEDGEMENTS

My gratitude goes to the editors of the following journals and anthologies in which stories and pieces from this book first appeared, sometimes in other forms: *Blotterature, Cortland Review, Eleven Eleven, Emprise Review, The Fabulist, The Fredericksburg Literary and Art Review, The Journal of Compressed Arts, museum of americana, Newfound Journal, The Quotable, RHINO, Staccato Fiction,* and *VOLT.*

"Fragmentation" appears in *Fragmentation and Other Stories,* ed. Jana Warning and Ryan Rivas, (Burrow Press, 2011). "Day of the Dead" appears in *50 Over 50,* (PS Books, 2016).

Thank you to Ariana D. Den Bleyker and ELJ Editions for being such good friends to writers.

Endless thanks to David Kroll for the use of his gorgeous painting "White Dove and Roses."

My deep gratitude to generous friends who read various versions of this book or its contents: Lauren Alwan, Mari Coates, Cheryl Dumesnil, Scott Landers, Kate Milliken, Charles Smith, Robert Thomas, Genanne Walsh, John Zic, Olga Zilberbourg, and especially to Tom Barbash, Molly Giles, Glen David Gold, Margot Livesey, Peter Orner, Melissa Pritchard, and Joan Silber.

Thank you to members of the North Bay Writers Workshop, who wrote along beside me and inspired me with their dedication to the art and the craft, and to my students over the years who have taught me so much.

I'm beyond lucky to have had these teachers: Karen Brennan, Kevin McIlvoy, Joan Silber, and Charles Wachtel. Ellen Bryant Voigt is a shining star whose encouragement made all the difference. And my deepest gratitude and love to Cass Pursell, for whom words aren't sufficient.

ABOUT THE AUTHOR

Peg Alford Pursell is the author of *Show Her a Flower, a Bird, a Shadow* (ELJ Editions). Her work has been published in *the Journal of Compressed Arts*, *RHINO*, *Forklift Ohio*, *VOLT*, among others, and shortlisted for the Flannery O'Connor Award. She founded and directs Why There Are Words, a national neighborhood of reading series, and is the director and founder of WTAW Press, an independent publisher of literary books. She lives in Northern California. http://www.pegalfordpursell.com